Vio Lets Go

NESMA SATTAR

Paperback ISBN: 978-981-18-4871-1
Hardcover ISBN: 978-981-18-4870-4

Puplic Library of Singapore

First Edition
2022

To every child holding this book right now,
I have written this book for you!

To Raja, Najatt, and Zeenat ♥

There once lived a violet-
sea-snail artist
in a faraway CONTINENT.

Gigantic to an ant but at-the-same-time so tiny to an ELEPHANT.

Her
**vivid,
vibrant,
violet**

color got her nothing but COMPLIMENT.

Oh dear, it's MAGNIFICENT!

Right where sea-waves
and shore-sands
have always met,
hid her town there
under a shiny fishnet.

Her name was VIO, her friends were slug BARROW,
three Sea-bunny triplets,
and Holo the LIMPET.

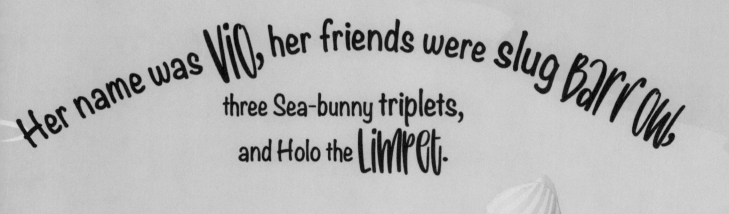

Vio's favorite color was violet,
her favorite shade was the lightest.

And so has become her ONLY choice when trying to be her best.

Vio and friends head to the **ice cream** shop for a little **refreshment**
Caramel, strawberry, chocolate chip?
Vio's **favorite** flavor was **mint**.

Still, she kept that as a **secret**,
and had something else to **select**.

She mixed **figs**, **grapes** and **eggplant**
to get her **favorite** shade **correct**!

Everyone was **done** in less than a **minute**,
but **no one** knew why **Vio** let hers **Melt**.

Everything's so stickily wet,
and so strangely SMELT!

She chose a huge **violet** card,
and a **violet** pen with a fresh lavender SCENT!

Everyone enjoyed **cards**-reading-time till the very last **MOMENT.**
Yet, no one knew why Holo's feelings were so **hurt**
or what Vio really **MEANT!**

An **empty** card? Oh no, it **isn't**!

Vio ordered mom a beautiful watch with a matching **bracelet.**

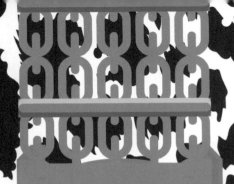

She asked the shop to make the case, hands, and dials all in light violet.

Everyone was home
from school on time,
except for Vio
who did not, yet!

No wonder she waited for mom so long,
now Vio is super upset.

It's Amusement Park Day

Vio and friends agreed to meet there at the opposite PAVEMENT.

She took the map, chose the only **violet** ride, and was sure 100%.

It's Contest Day

The day that Vio has **very much** been longing for **it**.
She went so ready with her all-**violet-shades** *palette*.

Contestants were asked to paint
Earth mountains during the sunset.

First Vio painted three little
mountains all in light violet.

But for some reason it looked so bad
in a way she did not EXPECT!

Then Vio looked up at the mountains' view
with a great awe of RESPECT.

Forgetting about her own **palette**,
Vio used the **pallete** her friends have quickly **sent**.

She dipped her **violet** brush in raven-**Black** till she no longer saw **violet**.

Such a one-of-a-kind **event**!

She repeated in shades of **Red**, and now her brush and **White** have finally **met**!

Those were the **mountains'** real **colors** that looked just **PERFECT!**

Very similar to many creatures
out there and far from any **defect.**

Vio's happiness when announced **winner**,
was to a full **extent.**
She jumped with joy and **proudly** went up to receive her **present.**

Her biggest **victory** for the day was learning to **accept** and appreciate what's **different**.

Everyone cheered for **Vio**, now they all know how hard it was for **Vio** to let **go**!

Questions

Why does Vio love Violet so much?

Why did Vio let her ice cream melt?

Why was Holo upset when she read Vio's Card?

Why was mommy so late for pick up?

Why did Vio ride the roller coaster alone?

Why did Vio change her painting?

What did Vio learn to let go?

Watch the animated book at
NESMASATTAR.COM

Have you found any creatures out there of the mountains' colors?
Connect with the Author about your findings on:
NESMASATTAR.COM